Hello, Family Members,

Learning to read is one of the most important accomplishments of early childhood. **Hello Reader!** books are designed to help children become skilled readers who like to read. Beginning readers learn to read by remembering frequently used words like "the," "is," and "and"; by using phonics skills to decode new words; and by interpreting picture and text clues. These books provide both the stories children enjoy and the structure they need to read fluently and independently. Here are suggestions for helping your child *before*, *during*, and *after* reading:

Before

- Look at the cover and pictures and have your child predict what the story is about.
- Read the story to your child.
- Encourage your child to chime in with familiar words and phrases.
- Echo read with your child by reading a line first and having your child read it after you do.

During

- Have your child think about a word he or she does not recognize right away. Provide hints such as "Let's see if we know the sounds" and "Have we read other words like this one?"
- Encourage your child to use phonics skills to sound out new words.
- Provide the word for your child when more assistance is needed so that he or she does not struggle and the experience of reading with you is a positive one.
- Encourage your child to have fun by reading with a lot of expression . . . like an actor!

After

- Have your child keep lists of interesting and favorite words.
- Encourage your child to read the books over and over again. Have him or her read to brothers, sisters, grandparents, and even teddy bears. Repeated readings develop confidence in young readers.
- Talk about the stories. Ask and answer questions. Share ideas about the funniest and most interesting characters and events in the stories.

I do hope that you and your child enjoy this book.

—Francie Alexander
Reading Specialist,
Scholastic's Instructional Publishing Group

For my Vermont Aunt Helen Martin McClausland
1909-1998
—J. Marzollo

To my confidantes: Kay, Ruth, Cheryl & Dale
—J. Moffatt

Cut-paper photography by Paul Dyer.

**Go to www.scholastic.com for Web site information
on Scholastic authors and illustrators.**

Text copyright © 1998 by Jean Marzollo.
Illustrations copyright © 1998 by Judith Moffatt.
All rights reserved. Published by Scholastic Inc.
SCHOLASTIC, HELLO READER! and CARTWHEEL BOOKS and associated
logos are trademarks and/or registered trademarks of Scholastic Inc.

Library of Congress Cataloging-in-Publication Data

Marzollo, Jean.
    I am snow / by Jean Marzollo; illustrated by Judith Moffatt.
      p.   cm. — (Hello reader! Science Level 1)
    Summary: Explains what snow is and what can be done with it.
Includes instructions for making a snowflake from paper.
    ISBN 0-590-64174-3
    1. Snow—Juvenile literature.   [1. Snow.]   I. Moffatt, Judith, ill.
    II. Title.   III. Series.
QC929.9.S7M37 1998
551.57'84—dc21   98-17757
                                                                                                              CIP
                                                                                                              AC

20 19 18   07
Printed in the U.S.A.   23
First printing, December 1998

I Am Snow

by Jean Marzollo
Illustrated by Judith Moffatt

Hello Reader! Science — Level 1

Cartwheel
·B·O·O·K·S·®

SCHOLASTIC INC.
New York Toronto London Auckland Sydney

I am not rain.
I do not drip,
         drip,
         drip.

I am not hail.
I do not bounce,
    bounce,
    bounce.

I am not ice.
I do not crack,
      crack,
        crack.

I am snow.
I fall gently,
      gently,
      gently.

I am a million,
billion, trillion
snowflakes
all piled up.

Each snowflake is
a crystal (KRIS-tal).
Each crystal has
six sides.
Catch one on your
mitten.
Are there six points?
Yes!

From afar,
all snowflakes look the same.
Up close,
you can see them better.
Each snowflake is different.

Some snow is wet
and sticky.
Wet snow makes good
snow people.

And snowballs!

Some snow is
dry and fluffy.
It is easy to shovel.

Who loves snow?
Skiers.
Snowboarders.

Snowshoe hikers.
Snow sliders.

Artists love snow, too.
This artist cut snowflakes
from tissue paper.
To find out how,
turn the page.

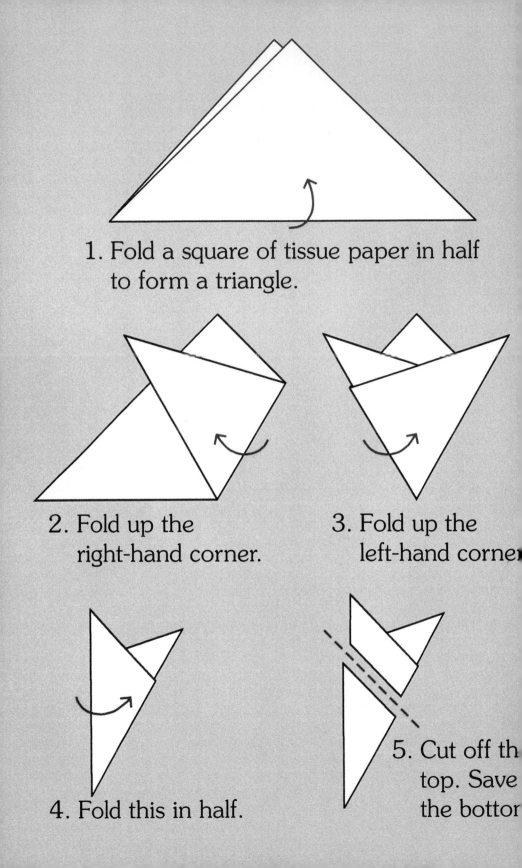

1. Fold a square of tissue paper in half
   to form a triangle.

2. Fold up the
   right-hand corner.

3. Fold up the
   left-hand corner

4. Fold this in half.

5. Cut off th
   top. Save
   the bottor

6. Cut away pieces from all three sides.

7. Open!

What happens
to cold snow
in warm weather?
It melts.

Just like the rain,
it goes drip,
       drip,
        drip.